SURPRISE!

CAROLINE HADILAKSONO

ARTHUR A. LEVINE BOOKS
An Imprint of Scholastic Inc.

Bear, Raccoon, and Squirrel had been friends for a really long time.

"I'm bored," said Squirrel.

"I wish there was something more exciting to do," said Raccoon.

"I wish we had new friends to play with," said Bear.

But making new friends . . .

. . . isn't always easy.

They waited a long time for the right friend
to wander into their neck of the woods.

One day, their wait was finally over.

They'd heard of city folks, but they'd never seen any, until now.

Eagerly, they hatched a plot to convince the city folks to stay. "We need to do something splendid," said Bear.

"How about a Welcome Party?" said Raccoon.
"Yes, a surprise Welcome Party," said Squirrel.

"We will have the most splendid foods," said Raccoon.

"And the most splendid entertainment," said Squirrel.

"And the most splendid decorations," said Bear.

They were almost ready.

"Hmm, something is missing. I will be right back," said Bear.

It wasn't long until Raccoon and Squirrel heard footsteps. But it wasn't Bear who returned.

"I made you the most splendid snacks," said Raccoon.

"I practiced my most splendid act," said Squirrel.

CHURP
CHIRP
CHURP

The surprise went just as they had hoped.
Their guests were perfectly shocked.

Finally, Bear returned . . .
with party hats for everyone!

But the guests were in a hurry to leave.

"Don't leave! We have the most splendid food!" said Raccoon.

"We have the most splendid entertainment!" said Squirrel.

"You forgot your party hats!" said Bear.

They didn't know why the city folks left so soon.
But Bear, Squirrel, and Raccoon had a splendid time
together, just the three of them.

For the lonely reader

All rights reserved.
Published by Arthur A. Levine Books, an imprint of Scholastic Inc.,
Publishers since 1920. SCHOLASTIC and the LANTERN LOGO
are trademarks and/or registered trademarks of Scholastic Inc.

The publisher does not have any control over and does not assume any responsibility
for author or third-party websites or their content.

Library of Congress Cataloging-in-Publication Data

Names: Hadilaksono, Caroline, author, illustrator.
Title: Surprise! / Caroline Hadilaksono.
Description: First edition. | New York, NY : Arthur A. Levine Books, an
imprint of Scholastic Inc., 2018. | Summary: Bear, Raccoon, and Squirrel
are good friends, and when some city folks visit their woods they plan to
throw a welcome party with snacks and entertainment—but when Bear
returns with the party hats the humans are suddenly in a hurry to leave.
Identifiers: LCCN 2017054168 | ISBN 9781338139198 (hardcover: alk. paper)
Subjects: LCSH: Forest animals—Juvenile fiction. | Human-animal
relationships—Juvenile fiction. | Friendship—Juvenile fiction. | CYAC:
Forest animals—Fiction. | Human-animal relationships—Fiction.
Friendship—Fiction. Classification: LCC PZ7.1.H224 Su 2018
DDC [E]—dc23 LC record available at https://lccn.loc.gov/2017054168

10 9 8 7 6 5 4 3 2 1   18 19 20 21 22

Printed in China   62

First edition, October 2018

The images in this book are a mix of watercolor paintings
and gouache textures, all combined and finished off digitally.
Book design by Christine Kettner